to Jill & Jim
& family

Ted & Nancy
Nypak!

from

Great tales to
out loud as
a family.

D1213998

Ivan the Fool

and Three Shorter Tales for Living Peaceably

HOLY FOOL ARTS

Ivan the Fool

and Three Shorter Tales for Living Peaceably

by
LEO TOLSTOY

Edited by
Ted Lewis

Translated by
Louise Maude
and **Aylmer Maude**

Foreword by
Jay Beck
and **Tevyn East**

A *Holy Fool Arts* Edition

WIPF *&* STOCK · Eugene, Oregon

IVAN THE FOOL AND THREE SHORTER TALES FOR LIVING PEACEABLY

Wipf & Stock
An Imprint of Wipf and Stock Publishers
199 W. 8th Ave., Suite 3
Eugene, OR 97401

www.wipfandstock.com

PAPERBACK ISBN: 978-1-5326-5494-7
HARDCOVER ISBN: 978-1-5326-5495-4
EBOOK ISBN: 978-1-5326-5496-1

Manufactured in the U.S.A.   05/25/18

The first collection in which *Ivan the Fool* appeared in Russian was *The Kreutzer Sonata and Other Stories* in 1890. After that, it appeared in the collections *Twenty-Three Tales* in 1905 and *Walk in the Light and Twenty-Three Other Tales* in 1906.

All four tales were translated into English by Louise and Aylmer Maude, and first published in *Twenty-Three Tales* (Oxford, 1928).

Contents

Foreword

"In the name of God, stop a moment, cease your work, look around you."
— Leo Tolstoy[1]

Tolstoy's desperate command in the quote above is perfectly suited to the challenges of the early 21st century. In an era that idolizes wealth and power, that inundates us with vile proclamations such as "time is money," and that defines 'maturity' and 'responsibility' in terms of economic prosperity (while denying that its pursuit has caused global climate change and massive inequality), the need to "cease our work and look around" is imperative. Of course, in the prevailing economic paradigm of global capitalism, this is a foolish act. But 'fools' have been trying to help us see through illusions from the beginning of time.

In this small but powerful collection of folk tales, you will meet Ivan and come to see how his actions, though considered foolish by many, help to unveil the reality behind the world's illusions and offer a glimpse of a different way of being. These stories draw on an ancient, archetypal motif, present in almost every culture, but known within Christendom as the Holy Fool. Often understood as a type of prophet, the Holy Fool veers sharply away from the status quo, embracing the seemingly ridiculous in order to reveal deep truths.

Holy Fools in Tolstoy's Russia, known as "yurodivy," were known for putting on eccentric displays of poverty, theatrical protest, and public nakedness, and yet were revered as divinely possessed devotees of Christ. A

1. Leo Tolstoy, *What is Art? & Wherein is Truth in Art?* (Meditations on Aesthetics & Literature) trans. Aylmer Maude, Louise Maude, Nathan Haskell Dole, & Isabel Hapgood (Musaicum Books, June 21, 2017), Kindle Edition.

vii

most beloved yurodivy, Basil the Blessed, for whom a cathedral in Moscow is named, is just one of many fools venerated in orthodox Christian traditions. These folks walked a thin line, serving people yet shunning recognition. They used a kind of performative madness to undermine any "respectability politics" and called into question the very notion of sanity.[2] As barefoot monks who scavenged for food, they illuminated the stigmas of poverty and the crimes of the mighty.

The practice of using foolish actions as a foil for societal dysfunction is certainly not original to these Russian holy men and women, but appears in cultural mythologies, folktales, religious figureheads, and festivals across the globe and throughout time. Wes Nisker suggests that Holy Fools rise from the fringes of society, but end up shaping the hearts of the great religions.[3] He includes Lao Tzu, Buddha, and Christ within their number. They each cherish an uncompromising commitment to live according to their deepest convictions, even if that means shirking social obligations and rejecting hierarchical structures. Nisker goes on to elaborate on the nuances of this tradition of "crazy wisdom" that ushers in absurdity, rebellion, and reversal through many types of holy foolery.

In Nisker's book, *The Essential Crazy Wisdom*, we meet and learn about the distinctive characters of Clown, Jester, Trickster, and Holy Fool. The Clown is familiar to us as the laughable buffoon with ridiculously exaggerated features and actions. The Clown's awkward stumbling mirrors our own frailty and ineptitude, seeding doubt in the midst of our misplaced confidence. The Jester is a master of wit and playful mockery, uniquely positioned to speak truth to power. Tasked with entertaining the king's court, he often finds himself in influential roles, compelling the ears of the elite. The Trickster is a boundary crosser who recreates worlds through transgressive actions; he breaks taboos, challenges concepts of right and wrong, and introduces new or competing paradigms. Each of these characters critique the prevailing socio-political framework; they poke, they prod, and they play, thereby calling dominant narratives into question. The last of these characters, however, the Holy Fool, completely obliterates the paradigm by acting outside of it. His presence beyond accepted systems and symbols

---

2. Eugene Vodolazkin, "Russian 'Umberto Eco' demystifies the Holy Fool" *Russia Beyond*, June 6, 2013, https://www.rbth.com/literature/2013/06/06/russian_umberto_eco_demystifies_the_holy_fool_26401.html

3. Wes Nisker, *The Essential Crazy Wisdom* (Toronto: Ten Speed Press, 2001), 54.

casts doubt not only on their power, but also on their very existence. He turns the world upside down and inside out.

The "powers that be" cannot allow such rebels to thrive, and thus these four expressions of "crazy wisdom" are in constant danger of being either destroyed or domesticated. The Church and State have utilized both strategies, working, on one hand, to discredit, demonize, or even outlaw Holy Fool outliers, or, alternatively, to co-opt them through appropriation and commodification. But despite proliferated attempts by the Church, the State, and the ruling class to eradicate these figures and their legacies, folk traditions worldwide have preserved these archetypal powers. Nisker writes:

> "The four archetypes share an uncanny ability to escape the trouble they inevitably get themselves into: the clown gets bopped, the trickster is dismembered and blown apart, the jester may have his head cut off by the king or be hit by rotten fruit thrown from the audience, and the great fool is about to fall off a cliff or be martyred by an angry mob. But just when it seems that all is lost, they rise again, recovered and whole, even from death. (The dismembered Coyote reassembles, Jesus Christ rises into everlasting life.) Because of their humor or their innocence, or because their revelations are so important, these crazy wisdom characters are immortal."[4]

The Holy Fool's message is recurrent throughout history, not because it is allowed a seat at the table of empire, but because those under the table or banished to the margins choose to celebrate it and keep it alive. (Notably, however, the fool is often given a seat of honor within indigenous and earth-honoring cultures, whose traditions involve sacred clowns and mythologies that revere the tricksters.)

Tolstoy's interest in the notion of "crazy wisdom" is evident in the way he approaches the telling of these folk tales. Tolstoy's spiritual awakening and radicalization process came through his reading of scripture, and particularly the gospel story, which inspired and rooted his anarchist views. Tolstoy's subsequent analysis around nonviolence influenced other Holy Fools, such as Gandhi and Martin Luther King, Jr. His Christian anarchism set itself against the institutions of both the Church and the State. Guardian writer Giles Fraser writes: "He was a thorn in the side of organized religion and, even more so, a vigorous opponent of the state. For Tolstoy, the state

---

4. Wes Nisker, *The Essential Crazy Wisdom* (Toronto: Ten Speed Press, 2001), 31.

was one great big protection racket, a monopoly of organized violence demanding money for a false promise of security. For by the raising of armies its citizens organize for war and yet also make themselves a target for attack. Thus the 'Christian' state is a contradiction in terms." [5] These bold stances stemmed from Tolstoy's reading of the gospel, which led him to despise hierarchical structures and power imbalances.

Let us remember, Tolstoy's subversive tale of *Ivan the Fool* (a peasant hero of Russian folklore[6]) was dreamed and embellished inside an imperial context. Tolstoy published this tale in 1886. Twenty-five years earlier, 20 million serfs were emancipated from a feudal system by the liberal reforms of Emperor Alexander II, which led to a surge of radical social analysis and revolutionary action. Two decades later, and five years before *Ivan the Fool* was published, Emperor Alexander II was assassinated, and imperial power transferred to his son Alexander III. This new tzar was an anti-Semitic nationalist who reversed his father's initiatives through repressive action; he forced the widespread adoption of one language and a solitary orthodox religion in order to squelch revolutionary unrest. The Russian Orthodox Church, awash in state power, officially excommunicated Tolstoy in 1901.

Tolstoy connected the wisdom of these folk tales to the subversive wisdom of the gospel, which, according to Tolstoy's reading, indicated that there should be no ruler. In the story of *Ivan the Fool*, Ivan's brothers, tempted by money and military power, seem destined to have the upper hand. Yet innocent Ivan, with his simple and unsuspecting ways, defeats the treacherous "devils" and gains a position of power as the fool king. The moral of these tales suggests that if there has to be a ruler, then it needs to be someone who doesn't have money, doesn't have an army, allows anybody in, helps his brothers even after they transgress, and rewards the meek. It is the world turned upside down. It is no spoiler to share that Ivan triumphs within this story; that is the way of most fairy tales. But we would be amiss to simplify this narrative into a children's morality tale and neglect its nuanced political implications.

In many folk tales, including the ones in this volume, the fool is pitted against characters who act as personifications of the dominant culture. It is important, therefore, to unpack the narrative function not only of Ivan's

5. Giles Fraser, "Tolstoy's Christian anarchism was a war on both church and state." *The Guardian*, Jan, 21, 2016, https://www.theguardian.com/commentisfree/belief/2016/jan/21/tolstoy-war-peace-christian-anarchism-church-state.

6. Andrei Sinyavsky, *Ivan the Fool: Russian Folk Belief: A Cultural History* (London/Moscow: GLAS New Russian Writing, 2007).

brothers, but also of the devil and his servants, the imps. The Christian church after Constantine derived many of its images of the Devil from ancient pagan representations of animal gods, in order to seed mistrust and doubt in those traditions. We think it is better to understand the "devil" and his "imps" in Tolstoy's tales as personifications of systemic injustice. Walter Wink's work on the biblical "principalities and powers" helps us see the spiritual significance of political and societal institutions and their role in the personal and political oppression.

In Ivan's adventures, we can glimpse the truth that "personal redemption cannot take place apart from the redemption of our social structures," as Wink writes.[7] He goes on to say: "The gospel, then, is not a message about the salvation of individuals from the world, but news about a world transfigured, right down to its basic structures."[8]

Ivan the Fool, like many other old folk tales, carries a legacy of longing for another world and offers an invitation for another way to be. We are grateful to be able to lean into these stories and listen again to the wisdom of the fool!

Tevyn East and Jay Beck
April 2018
Philadelphia

7. Walter Wink, *Unmasking the Powers: The Invisible Forces That Determine Human Existence* (Philadelphia: Fortress Press, 1986), 98.

8. Walter Wink, *The Powers That Be: Theology for a New Millennium* (New York: Doubleday, April 1998), 36.

Introduction

It is quite an irony that an author who produced titanic novels such as *War and Peace* and *Anna Karenina* could, in later years, write simple folk tales for young readers. On one hand Leo Tolstoy (1828–1910) exposed humanity's darkest motives and duplicities, while on the other hand he elevated the human capacity for living simply and peaceably in a better future. One way to make sense of this tension is to distinguish phases in his literary vocation. Much has been made of Tolstoy's spiritual 'turn' in his later years which resulted in writings characterized by a moralistic and didactic tone. It appears at some point that he forsook his earlier, nuanced view of human nature to promote a more idealistic vision of what society could become.

A case for continuity, however, can be made, as Raymond Rosenthal did in his introduction to *Leo Tolstoy: Fables and Fairy Tales* (1962).[1] He noted Tolstoy's indebtedness to his eldest brother Nikolai who steeped the younger in a world of virtue-ladened fairy-tale. This fantasy world included a buried green stick near Tolstoy's boyhood home. His brother would speak of a secret message written on the stick that would destroy all evils and make all people happy. Love would someday turn the world into a golden age. One sign of Tolstoy's lifelong devotion to this ideal is that he requested to be buried by this green stick in the Zakaz Forest.

Whether or not the aging Tolstoy can be understood as a contradiction with his past selves is best left to the scholars. What is evident is that in the years following his completion of *Anna Karenina* (1886) he decidedly took on stronger commitments to a number of radical orientations, including asceticism, anarchism, pacifism, anti-institutionalism (of both religion and government), and the rejection of private land ownership.

1. Raymond Rosenthal, Introduction to *Leo Tolstoy: Fables and Fairy Tales* (Signet Classic, New American Library, 1962).

These themes increasingly found expression in his non-fictional writings. Nevertheless, Tolstoy did manage to infuse his growing radicalism into a set of tales geared for peasants and school children.

The tales in this volume hang on two social critiques aimed at militarism and materialism. *Ivan the Fool* (1886) combines both critiques as represented by the pursuits of Ivan's two brothers. *Esarhaddon, King of Assyria* (1903) echoes the judgment on military power, and *A Grain as Big as a Hen's Egg* (1866) does the same for unsustainable economies. *Ivan the Fool* is also significant in its connection to the older Russian tradition of the Holy Fool. The final story, *Three Questions* (1885; 1903), serves to enrich the role of the Holy Fool in this collection.

Rosenthal points out an interesting contrast between classic fairy tales and Tolstoy's tales. In the former, main characters rely on their evolving inner virtues to overcome various obstacles and thereby receive the gold or happiness that they finally get in the end. "In Tolstoy's tales, however, the hero's humility and kindness are simply the preconditions for the achievement of a greater wisdom and self-awareness, and his reward is never wealth or personal success but rather his ability to conquer, both for himself and others, a new and deeper area of human value and responsibility."[2]

Here we can see a strong connection with the Holy Fool. What makes this figure 'holy', in the Russian tradition, is precisely this element of *precondition*. Such a person is already, as Jesus said, "like a child" who lives and moves according to the moral order of the Kingdom of God. The fool, in an upside down sense, has already arrived and thus leads others into this kingdom of "human value and responsibility." Not only does the fool have little use for gold, as we see at the end of the Ivan story, but the common folk who share in this holy foolery end up lampooning the value of gold itself. Similarly, we find the same uselessness regarding soldiers and weaponry.

Does this mean we either have or do not have an innate capacity to be care-free within ourselves or to freely care for the welfare of others? Not at all. Human choice to change within is still vital. Tolstoy wanted to stimulate the best within people so they could act out of love and courage for the good of those around them. And most often, acting according to higher principles takes a bit of risk. We typically restrain ourselves out of fear. It may even seem foolish to perform an act of random kindness or to live completely in the present. But that is precisely why we are confronted with the paradoxical wisdom of the Holy Fool.

2. Rosenthal, *Fables*, p. xii.

One way to think about Tolstoy's use of the folk-fairy tale to poke at institutionalized powers and mindsets is to see a parallel in Jesus' encounter with the rich young ruler. There we find the same upsetting language about wealth and status while also experiencing humorous hyperbole. "It is easier for a camel to enter an eye of a needle than for a rich person to enter God's kingdom" (Mark 10:25). Something more than moralism is going on here. A playful yet probing genre that sticks in the mind is sometimes the only genre that can 'needle' human hearts to change. And such it is with tales that playfully push to the extremes.

Esarhaddon, King of Assyria strikes an important chord for us as themes of violence and victimization receive increasing attention in today's world. Esarhaddon, reigning from 681 to 669 BC, comes at the end of a long line of Assyrian kings known for ruthless violence in treating rebels and displaced populations.[3] Prior to the Babylonian destruction of Jerusalem and the deportation of Judean Jews, the Assyrians were the dominant superpower of the day. Why then did Tolstoy choose this particular monarch? The best clue comes from Ernest Budge's *History of Esarhaddon*,[4] published in 1880, which records an episode of the vassal king Lailie asking Esarhaddon to restore his nation's captured gods. Esarhaddon granted the request, saying, "I spoke to him of brotherhood, and entrusted to him the sovereignty of the districts of Bazu." In this we see the seeds of a story which, for Tolstoy, could portray an awakening of empathy.

A Grain as Big as a Hen's Egg integrates themes of bodily health, work ethics, and economic sustainability. Again, we face the impulse to dismiss the moral lessons of this tale due to the exaggerated idealism of peasant culture. One thinks of classic attempts to dismiss the practicality of Jesus' teachings in the Sermon on the Mount. Tolstoy, however, is helping us to see the vital weave between several interlocking areas of human life: health, nutrition, agriculture, labor, and social relations. By using health and aging as an outcome measure of this matrix, he prompts us to confront the tragic weave of comparable areas in modern life: poor health, poor nutrition, poor soil, along with industrial farming and money-based mega-economies. Undergirding the entire discussion, for Tolstoy, are the positive virtues of contentment and hard work.

---

3. In the Hebrew Bible, see 2 Kings 17:24; 19:28; 2 Chronicles 33:11; Isaiah 37:38; Ezra 4:2.

4. Earnest A. Budge, *The History of Esarhaddon* (London: Trubner, 1880).

The *Three Questions* pokes a bit at a society's general inability to discern the most important things in life. The story highlights two top ideals for Tolstoy: living mindfully in the present and living in service to others. The wise hermit, like the Holy Fool, has a precedent in Russian history which owes something, in part, to the Desert Fathers and Mothers. (In fact, if you were to google "hermit in Russia" under online Images, you will see for yourself that this tradition is still alive and well.) Related to this is the *poustinia*, a Russian word meaning 'desert' or 'wilderness'; more specifically, it designates a modest hut or cabin where a hermit lives and prays.[5] One ultimately has to ask why the king is drawn to such a marginalized spot to find the wisdom he seeks, and thus we find ourselves likewise drawn to the margins.

Returning again to *Ivan the Fool*, we recognize how the respective elements in the three shorter tales can all be found in the story of Ivan. For that very reason they were chosen for this volume. In addition to the prevalence of violent and commercial mindsets in today's modern world, it is worth recalling that Martin Luther King, Jr. named a third 'ism' among his critiques of militarism and materialism, namely racism. All three leave large segments of the human family living vulnerably on the margins of any mega-society, and it is precisely in those margins that voices can rise up and be heard. The reason such voices sound *foolish* is because they do not represent the interests of the status quo. But they often do represent a way of living peaceably.

Tolstoy saw how Russia's imperial trends in the 19th century were eroding the agrarian peasant culture with which he had close association. In this context, local peasants provided Tolstoy with not only an audience but also a source of material for his tales. He understood how the worlds of fairy tale and peasantry were closely connected, not unlike the way tribal cultures make close association between spirit and nature. As mentioned above, Tolstoy clearly idealized peasant culture in his tales. But this should not prevent us from seeing how peasant cultures have a closer affinity to both the archetypal and moral richness reflected in these tales.

One of his students recounted the time Tolstoy read his newly finished "Ivan the Fool" story to a local group of peasants, asking one of them to repeat it back in his own words. This peasant modified the story a fair amount. Nevertheless, Tolstoy was delighted by the adaption, jotted down

---

5. Catherine de Hueck Doherty, *Poustinia: Encountering God in Silence, Solitude and Prayer* (Ogdensburg, NY: Madonna House Publications, 1975/2000).

the changes, and then published the tale in the revised form. Later he told the student that this was a common practice, since for him it was "the only way to write stories for the people."[6] In this way, we can hear, though faintly, the marginalized voice of the peasant.

Ultimately these tales, like a good parable, entertain well and teach well simultaneously. In fact, parables, as suggested by the literal meaning of the word, 'throw us beyond' our normal ways of thinking. By juxtaposing our current conventions with new possibilities, Tolstoy's tales snag and carry us into new places. In the end, peasants with calluses on their hands eat first and the intellectuals eat the leftovers. The real question we are all left with is whether we can allow ourselves to move beyond our heads, into our hearts, and finally through our hands.

Ted Lewis

April 2018

Duluth, MN

Editorial note: Throughout the translation of these tales by Louise and Aylmer Maude, I have taken the liberty to make slight modifications to improve the text for today's readers. These changes include deleting unnecessary commas, replacing numerous semicolons with commas or periods, changing 'till' to 'until', removing the hyphen from 'to-morrow', removing the British 'u' from words like 'labour', and occasionally adding or changing a word to strengthen a sentence. Double-quotes have also been uniformly added.

---

6. Rosenthal, *Fables*, p. xv.

The Story of Iván the Fool

Part 1

Once upon a time, in a certain province of a certain country, there lived a rich peasant who had three sons: Simon the Soldier, Tarás the Stout, and Iván the Fool, besides an unmarried daughter, Milania, who was deaf and dumb. Simon the Soldier went to the wars to serve the king, Tarás the Stout went to a city and became a merchant, and Iván the Fool stayed at home with the lass to till the ground until his back bent.

Simon the Soldier obtained high rank and an estate, and married a nobleman's daughter. His pay was large and his estate was large, but yet he could not make ends meet. What the husband earned his wife squandered, and they never had money enough.

So Simon the Soldier went to his estate to collect the income, but his steward said, "Where is any income to come from? We have neither cattle, nor tools, nor horse, nor plow, nor harrow. We must first get all these things and then the money will come."

Then Simon the Soldier went to his father and said, "You, father, are rich, but have given me nothing. Divide what you have and give me a third part that I may improve my estate."

But the old man said: "You brought nothing into my house; why should I give you a third part? It would be unfair to Iván and to the girl."

But Simon answered, "He is a fool, and she is an old maid, and deaf and dumb besides; what's the good of property to them?"

The old man said, "We will see what Iván says about it."

And Iván said, "Let him take what he wants."

So Simon the Soldier took his share of his father's goods and removed them to his estate, and went off again to serve the king.

Tarás the Stout also gathered much money, and married into a merchant's family, but still he wanted more. So he, also, came to his father and said, "Give me my portion."

But the old man did not wish to give Tarás a share either, and said, "You brought nothing here. Iván has earned all we have in the house, and why should we wrong him and the girl?"

But Tarás said, "What does he need? He is a fool! He cannot marry, for no one would have him, and the dumb lass does not need anything either. Look here, Iván!" said he. "Give me half the corn, for I don't want the tools; and of the livestock I will take only the grey stallion, which is of no use to you for the plow."

Iván laughed and said, "Take what you want. I will work to earn some more."

So they gave a share to Tarás also, and he carted the corn away to town and took the grey stallion. And Iván was left with one old mare to lead his peasant life as before and to support his father and mother.

Part 2

Now the old Devil was vexed that the brothers had not quarreled over the division but had parted peacefully, and so he summoned three imps.

"Look here," he said. "There are three brothers: Simon the Soldier, Tarás the Stout, and Iván the Fool. They should have quarreled, but they are living peaceably and meeting on friendly terms. The fool Iván has spoiled the whole business for me. Now you three go and tackle those three brothers, and worry them until they scratch each other's eyes out! Do you think you can do it?"

"Yes, we'll do it," they said.

"How will you set about it?"

"Why," said they, "first we'll ruin them. And when they haven't a crust to eat we'll tie them up together, and then they'll fight each other, sure enough!"

"That's capital! I see you understand your business. Go, and don't come back until you've set them by the ears, or I'll skin you alive!"

The imps went off into a swamp and began to consider how they should set to work. They disputed and disputed, each wanting the lightest job; but at last they decided to cast lots over which of the brothers each imp should tackle. If one imp finished his task before the others, he was to come and help them. So the imps cast lots and appointed a time to meet again in the swamp to learn who had succeeded and who needed help.

The appointed time came around, and the imps met again in the swamp as agreed. And each began to tell how matters stood. The first, who had undertaken Simon the Soldier, began by saying, "My business is going on well. Tomorrow Simon will return to his father's house."

His comrades asked, "How did you manage it?"

"First," says he, "I made Simon so bold that he offered to conquer the whole world for his king, and the king made him his general and sent him to fight the king of India. They met for battle, but the night before, I damped all the powder in Simon's camp and made more straw soldiers for the Indian king than you could count. And when Simon's soldiers saw the straw soldiers surrounding them, they grew frightened. Simon ordered them to fire, but their cannons and guns would not go off. Then Simon's soldiers were quite frightened and ran like sheep, and the Indian king slaughtered them. Simon was disgraced. He has been deprived of his estate, and tomorrow they intend to execute him. There is only one day's work left for me to do; I have just to let him out of prison that he may escape home. Tomorrow I shall be ready to help whichever of you needs me."

Then the second imp, who had Tarás in hand, began to tell how he had fared. "I don't want any help," said he. "My job is going alright. Tarás can't hold out for more than a week. First I caused him to grow greedy and fat. His covetousness became so great that whatever he saw he wanted to buy. He has spent all his money in buying immense quantities of goods, and he still continues to buy. Already he has begun to use borrowed money. His debts hang like a weight round his neck, and he is so involved that he can never get clear. In a week his bills come due, and before then I will spoil all his stock. He will be unable to pay and will have to go home to his father."

Then they asked the third imp about Iván the Fool. "And how are you getting on?" they asked.

"Well," said he, "my affair goes badly. First I spat into his drink to make his stomach ache, and then I went into his field and hammered the ground hard as a stone that he should not be able to till it. I thought he wouldn't plow it, but like the fool he is, he came with his plow and began to make a furrow. He groaned with the pain in his stomach, but went on plowing. I broke his plow for him, but he went home, got out another, and again started plowing. I crept under the earth and caught hold of the plowshares, but there was no holding them; he leant heavily upon the plow, and the plowshare was sharp and cut my hands. He has all but finished plowing the field; only one little strip is left. Come, brothers, and help me. For if we don't get the better of him, all our labor is lost. If the fool holds out and keeps on working the land, his brothers will never know want, for he will feed them both."

Simon the Soldier's imp promised to come the next day to help, and so they parted.

Part 3

Iván had plowed up the whole fallow field, but for one little strip. He came to finish it. Though his stomach ached, the plowing must be done. He freed the harness ropes, turned the plow, and began to work. He drove one furrow, but coming back the plow began to drag as if it had caught in a root. It was the imp, who had twisted his legs round the plowshare and was holding it back.

"What a strange thing!" thought Iván. "There were no roots here at all, and yet here's a root."

Iván pushed his hand deep into the furrow, groped about, and, feeling something soft, seized hold of it and pulled it out. It was black like a root, but it wriggled. Why, it was a live imp!

"What a nasty thing!" said Iván, and he lifted his hand to dash it against the plow, but the imp squealed out:

"Don't hurt me, and I'll do anything you tell me to."

"What can you do?"

"Anything you tell me to."

Iván scratched his head.

"My stomach aches," said he. "Can you cure that?"

"Certainly I can."

"Well then, do so."

The imp went down into the furrow, searched about, scratched with his claws, and pulled out a bunch of three little roots, which he handed to Iván.

"Here," said the imp. "Whoever swallows one of these will be cured of any illness."

Iván took the roots, separated them, and swallowed one. The pain in his stomach was cured at once. The imp again begged to be let off. "I will jump right into the earth and never come back."

"All right," said Iván. "Begone, and God be with you!"

And as soon as Iván mentioned God, the imp plunged into the earth like a stone thrown into the water. Only a hole was left.

Iván put the other two pieces of root into his cap and went on with his plowing. He plowed the strip to the end, turned his plow over, and went home. He unharnessed the horse, entered the hut, and there he saw his elder brother, Simon the Soldier with his wife, sitting at supper. Simon's estate had been confiscated, and he himself had barely managed to escape from prison, and so he had come back to live in his father's house.

Simon saw Iván and said: "I have come to live with you. Feed me and my wife until I get another appointment."

"All right," said Iván, "you can stay with us."

But when Iván was about to sit down on the bench, the lady disliked the smell and said to her husband: "I cannot sup with a dirty peasant."

So Simon the Soldier said, "My lady says you don't smell nice. You'd better go and eat outside."

"All right," said Iván. "It is all the same to me, for I must spend the night outside to pasture the mare."

So he took some bread, grabbed his coat, and went with the mare into the fields.

Part 4

Having finished his work that night, Simon's imp came, as agreed, to find Iván's imp and help him to subdue the fool. He came to the field and searched and searched; but instead of finding his comrade he found only a hole.

"Clearly," thought he, "some evil has befallen my comrade. I must take his place. The field is plowed up, so the fool must be tackled in the meadow."

So the imp went to the meadows and flooded Iván's hayfield with water, which left the grass all covered with mud.

Iván returned from the pasture at dawn, sharpened his scythe, and went to mow the hayfield. He began to mow, but had only swung the scythe once or twice when the edge turned blunt so that it would not cut at all, as it needed resharpening. Iván struggled on for a while, and then said: "It's no good. I must go home and bring a tool to sharpen the scythe. Besides, I'll get a chunk of bread at the same time. If I have to spend a week here, I won't leave until the mowing is done."

The imp heard this and thought to himself, "This fool is a tough one; I can't get around him this way. I must try some other dodge."

Iván returned, sharpened his scythe, and began to mow. The imp crept into the grass and began to catch the scythe by the heel, sending the point into the earth. Iván found the work very hard, but he mowed the whole meadow, except for one little bit which was in the swamp. The imp crept into the swamp and, thinking to himself, "Though I cut my paws, I will not let him mow."

Iván reached the swamp. The grass didn't seem thick, but yet it resisted the scythe. Iván grew angry and began to swing the scythe with all his might. The imp had to give in; he could not keep up with the scythe, and, seeing it was a bad business, he scrambled into a bush. Iván swung the scythe, caught the bush, and cut off half the imp's tail. Then Iván finished mowing the grass, told his sister to rake it up, and went himself to mow the rye. He went with the scythe, but the dock-tailed imp was there first, entangling the rye so that the scythe was of no use. But Iván went home and got his sickle, and began to reap with his new tool, and he reaped the whole of the rye.

"Now it's time," said he, "to start on the oats."

The dock-tailed imp heard this, and thought, "I couldn't get the better of him on the rye, but I shall on the oats. Only wait until the morning."

In the morning the imp hurried to the oat field, but the oats were already mowed down! Iván had mowed them by night in order that less grain should shake out and be lost. The imp grew angry.

"He has cut me all over and tired me out—the fool. It is worse than war. The accursed fool never sleeps; one can't keep up with him. I will get into his stacks now and rot them."

So the imp entered the rye and crept among the sheaves, and they began to rot. He heated the sheaves, grew warm himself, and fell asleep.

Iván harnessed the mare and went with the lass to cart the rye. He came to the heaps and began to pitch the rye into the cart. He tossed two sheaves and again thrust his fork, but this time it went right into the imp's back! He lifted the fork and saw on the prongs a live imp: dock-tailed, struggling, wriggling, and trying to jump.

"What, you nasty thing. Are you here again?"

6

"I'm another," said the imp. "The first was my brother. I've been with your brother Simon."

"Well," said Iván, "whoever you are, you've met the same fate!"

He was about to dash him against the cart, but the imp cried out: "Let me off, and I will not only let you alone, but I'll do anything you tell me to do."

"What can you do?"

"I can make soldiers out of anything you like."

"But what use are they?"

"You can turn them to any use; they can do anything you please."

"Can they sing?"

"Yes, if you want them to."

"All right. You may make me some."

And the imp said, "Here, take a sheaf of rye, then bump it upright on the ground, and simply say:

> 'O sheaf! my slave
> This order gave:
> Where a straw has been
> Let a soldier be seen!'"

Iván took the sheaf, struck it on the ground, and said what the imp had told him to. The sheaf fell apart and all the straws changed into soldiers, with a trumpeter and a drummer playing in front of a whole regiment.

Iván laughed. "How clever!" he said. "This is fine! How pleased the girls will be!"

"Now let me go," said the imp.

"No," said Iván, "I must turn my soldiers back into threshed straw, otherwise good grain will be wasted. Teach me how to change them back again into the sheaf. I want to thresh it."

And the imp told him to repeat this verse:

> "Let each be a straw
> Who was soldier before,
> For my true slave
> This order gave!'"

Iván said this, and the sheaf reappeared.

Again the imp began to beg, "Now let me go!"

"All right." And Iván pressed him against the side of the cart, held him down with his hand, and pulled him off the fork. "God be with you," he said.

And as soon as he mentioned God, the imp plunged into the earth like a stone into water. Only a hole was left.

Iván returned home, and there was his other brother, Tarás with his wife, sitting at supper.

Tarás the Stout had failed to pay his debts, had run away from his creditors, and had come home to his father's house. When he saw Iván, he said, "Look here. Until I can start in business again, I want you to keep me and my wife."

"All right," said Iván, "you can live here, if you like."

Iván took off his coat and sat down to table, but the merchant's wife said: "I cannot sit at table with this clown. He smells of perspiration."

Then Tarás the Stout said, "Iván, you smell too strong. Go and eat outside."

"All right," said Iván, taking some bread and going into the yard. "It is time, anyhow, for me to go and pasture the mare."

Part 5

Tarás's imp, being also free that night, came, as agreed, to help his comrades subdue Iván the Fool. He came to the cornfield, looked and looked for his comrades, but no one was there. He only found a hole. He went to the meadow, and there he found an imp's tail in the swamp, and another hole in the rye stubble.

"Evidently, some ill-luck has befallen my comrades," thought he. "I must take their place and tackle the fool."

So the imp went to look for Iván, who had already stacked the corn and was cutting trees in the wood. The two brothers had begun to feel crowded, living together, and thus they had told Iván to cut down trees to build new houses for them.

The imp ran to the wood, climbed among the branches, and began to hinder Iván from felling the trees. Iván undercut one tree so that it should fall clear, but in falling it turned askew and caught among some branches. Iván cut a pole with which to lever it aside, and with difficulty contrived to bring it to the ground. He set to work to fell another tree; again the same thing occurred, and with all his efforts he could hardly get the tree clear. He began on a third tree, and again the same thing happened.

Iván had hoped to cut down half a hundred small trees, but had not felled even half a score, and now the night had come and he was tired out.

8

The steam from him spread like a mist through the wood, but still he stuck to his work. He undercut another tree, but his back began to ache so that he could not stand. He drove his axe into the tree and sat down to rest.

The imp, noticing that Iván had stopped work, grew cheerful.

"At last," he thought, "he is tired out! He will give it up. Now I can take a rest myself."

He seated himself astride a branch of the same tree and chuckled. But soon Iván got up, pulled the axe out, swung it, and smote the tree from the opposite side with such force that the tree gave way at once and came crashing down. The imp had not expected this, and had no time to get his feet clear, and the tree, having been felled, trapped his leg. Iván began to lop off the branches, when he noticed a live imp stuck in the tree! Iván was surprised.

"What, you nasty thing," he said. "So you are here again!"

"I am another one," said the imp. "I have been with your brother Tarás."

"Whoever you are, you have met your fate," said Iván, and swinging his axe he was about to strike him with the haft, but the imp begged for mercy: "Don't strike me," said he, "and I will do anything you tell me to."

"What can you do?"

"I can make money for you, as much as you want."

"All right, make some." So the imp showed him how to do it.

"Take some leaves from this oak and rub them in your hands, and gold will fall out on the ground."

Iván took some leaves and rubbed them, and gold ran down from his hands.

"This stuff will do fine," he said, "for the fellows to play with on their holidays."

"Now let me go." said the imp.

"All right," said Iván, and taking a lever he set the imp free. "Now be-gone! And God be with you," he said.

And as soon as he mentioned God, the imp plunged into the earth like a stone into water. Only a hole was left.

Part 6

So the brothers built houses and began to live apart. And Iván finished the harvest work, brewed beer, and invited his brothers to spend the next holiday with him. His brothers would not come, though.

"We don't care about peasant feasts," they said.

So Iván entertained the peasants and their wives, and drank until he was rather tipsy. Then he went into the street to a ring of dancers, and going up to them he told the women to sing a song in his honor, "For," he said, "I will give you something you never saw in your lives before!"

The women laughed and sang his praises, and when they had finished they said, "Now let us have your gift."

"I will bring it directly," said he.

He took a seed-basket and ran into the woods. The women laughed. "He is a fool!" they said, and they began to talk of something else.

But soon Iván came running back, carrying the basket full of something heavy.

"Shall I give it to you?"

"Yes! Give it to us."

Iván took a handful of gold and threw it to the women. You should have seen them throw themselves upon it to pick it up! And the men around scrambled for it and snatched it from one another. One old woman was nearly crushed to death. Iván laughed.

"Oh, you fools!" he said. "Why did you crush the old grandmother? Be quiet, and I will give you some more," and he threw them some more. The people all crowded around, and Iván threw them all the gold he had. They asked for more, but Iván said, "I have no more just now. Another time I'll give you some more. Now let us dance, and you can sing me your songs."

The women began to sing.

"Your songs are no good," said Ivan.

"Where will you find better ones?" they asked.

"I'll soon show you," he said.

He went to the barn, took a sheaf, threshed it, stood it up, and bumped it on the ground.

"Now," said he:

> "O sheaf! my slave
> This order gave:
> Where a straw has been
> Let a soldier be seen!"

And the sheaf fell apart and became so many soldiers. The drums and trumpets began to play. Iván ordered the soldiers to play and sing. He led them out into the street and the people were amazed. The soldiers played and sang, and then Iván (forbidding any one to follow him) led them back to the threshing ground, changed them into a sheaf again, and threw the sheaf in its place.

He then went home and lay down in the stables to sleep.

Part 7

Simon the Soldier heard of all these things next morning and went to his brother.

"Tell me," he said, "where you got those soldiers from, and where you have taken them to?"

"What does it matter to you?" said Iván.

"What does it matter? Why, with soldiers one can do anything. One can win a kingdom."

Iván wondered with amazement.

"Really!" said he. "Why didn't you say so before? I'll make you as many as you like. It's a good thing the lass and I have threshed so much straw."

Iván took his brother to the barn and said: "Look here. If I make you some soldiers, you must take them away at once, for if we have to feed them, they will eat up the whole village in a day."

Simon the Soldier promised to lead the soldiers away, and so Iván began to make them. He bumped a sheaf on the threshing floor, and suddenly a company appeared. He bumped another sheaf, and there was a second company. He made so many that they covered the field.

"Will that do?" he asked.

Simon was overjoyed, and said, "That will do! Thank you, Iván!"

"All right," said Iván. "If you want more, come back, and I'll make them. There is plenty of straw this season."

Simon the Soldier at once took command of his army, collected and organized it, and went off to make war.

Hardly had Simon the Soldier gone, when Tarás the Stout came along. He, too, had heard of yesterday's affair, and he said to his brother: "Show me where you get gold money! If I only had some to start with, I could make it bring me in more money from all over the world."

Iván was astonished.

"Really!" said he. "You should have told me sooner. I will make you as much as you like."

His brother was delighted.

"Give me three full baskets to begin with."

"All right," said Iván. "Come into the forest. Or better still, let us harness the mare, for you won't be able to carry it all."

They drove to the forest, and Iván began to rub the oak leaves. He made a great heap of gold.

"Will that do?"

Tarás was overjoyed.

"It will do for the present," he said. "Thank you, Iván!"

"All right," says Iván. "If you want more, come back for it. There are plenty of leaves left."

Tarás the Stout gathered up a whole cartload of money and went off to trade.

So the two brothers went away: Simon to fight and Tarás to buy and sell. Simon the Soldier conquered a kingdom for himself, and Tarás the Stout made much money in trade.

When the two brothers met, each told the other about their accomplishments: Simon, as to how he got the soldiers, and Tarás, as to how he got the money. And Simon the Soldier said to his brother, "I have conquered a kingdom and live in grand style, but I have not money enough to keep my soldiers." And Tarás the Stout said, "I have made much money, but the trouble is, I have no one to guard it."

Then said Simon the Soldier, "Let us go to our brother. I will tell him to make more soldiers, and will then give them to you to guard your money, and you can tell him to make money for me to feed my men."

And thus they drove away to Iván. Simon then said, "Dear brother, I have not enough soldiers. Make me another couple of ricks or so."

Iván shook his head.

"No!" said he, "I will not make any more soldiers."

"But you promised you would."

"I know I promised, but I won't make any more."

"But why not, fool?"

"Because your soldiers killed a man. I was plowing the other day near the road, and I saw a woman taking a coffin along in a cart, and she was crying. I asked her who was dead. She said, 'Simon's soldiers have killed my husband in the war.' I thought the soldiers would only play tunes, but they have killed a man. I won't give you any more."

And he stuck to it and would not make any more soldiers.

Tarás the Stout, too, began to beg Iván to make him more gold money. But Iván shook his head.

"No, I won't make any more," said he.

"Didn't you promise?"

"I did, but I'll make no more," he said.

"Why not, fool?"

"Because your gold coins took away the cow from Michael's daughter."

"How?"

"Simply took it away! Michael's daughter had a cow. Her children used to drink the milk. But the other day her children came to me to ask for milk. I said, 'Where's your cow?' They answered, 'The steward of Tarás the Stout came and gave our mother three bits of gold, and she gave him the cow, so we have nothing to drink.' I thought you were only going to play with the gold pieces, but you have taken the children's cow away. I will not give you any more."

And Iván stuck to it and would not give him any more.

So the brothers went away. And as they went they discussed how they could meet their difficulties. And Simon said:

"Look here, I will tell you what to do. You give me money to feed my soldiers, and I will give you half my kingdom with soldiers enough to guard your money." Tarás agreed. So the brothers divided what they possessed, and both became kings, and both became rich.

Part 8

Iván lived at home, supporting his father and mother and working in the fields with his deaf and dumb sister. Now it happened that Iván's watchdog fell sick, grew mangy, and was near dying. Iván, pitying it, got some bread from his sister, put it in his cap, carried it out, and threw it to the dog. But the cap was torn, and together with the bread, one of the little roots fell to the ground. The old dog ate it up with the bread, and as soon as she had swallowed it she jumped up and began to play, bark, and wag her tail. In short, she became quite well again.

The father and mother saw it and were amazed.

"How did you cure the dog?" asked they.

Iván answered: "I had two little roots to cure any pain and she swallowed one."

Now about that time it happened that the King's daughter fell ill, and the King proclaimed in every town and village that he would reward anyone who could heal her, and if any unmarried man could heal the King's daughter he should have her for his wife. This was proclaimed in Iván's village as well as everywhere else.

His father and mother called Iván, and said to him: "Have you heard what the King has proclaimed? You said you had a root that would cure any sickness. Go and heal the King's daughter and you will be made happy for life."

"All right," he said.

Iván prepared to go, and they dressed him in his best. But as he went out of the door he met a beggar woman with a crippled hand.

"I have heard," said she, "that you can heal people. I pray that you cure my arm, for I cannot even put on my boots myself."

"All right," said Iván, and giving the little root to the beggar woman he told her to swallow it. She swallowed it and was cured. She was at once able to move her arm freely.

His father and mother came out to accompany Iván to the King, but when they heard that he had given away the root, and that he had nothing left to cure the King's daughter with, they began to scold him.

"You pity a beggar woman, but are not sorry for the King's daughter!" they said. But Iván felt sorry for the King's daughter also. So he harnessed the horse, put straw in the cart to sit on, and sat down to drive away.

"Where are you going, fool?"

"To cure the King's daughter."

"But you've nothing left to cure her with?"

"Never mind," said he, and drove off.

He drove to the King's palace, and as soon as he stepped on the threshold the King's daughter got well.

The King was delighted and had Iván brought to him; he then had Iván dressed in fine robes.

"Be my son-in-law," said the King.

"All right," said Iván.

And Iván married the princess. Her father died soon after, and Iván became king of the land. So all three brothers were now kings.

Part 9

The three brothers lived and reigned. The eldest brother, Simon the Soldier, prospered. With his straw soldiers he levied real soldiers. He ordered throughout his whole kingdom a levy of one soldier from every ten houses, and each soldier had to be tall, and also clean in body and in face. He gathered many such soldiers and trained them, and when any one opposed him, he sent his soldiers at once to get his own way. In this way, everyone began to fear him, and yet his life was a comfortable one. Whatever he cast his eyes on and wished for was his. He sent soldiers, and they brought him all he desired.

Tarás the Stout also lived comfortably. He did not waste the money he got from Iván, but increased it largely. He introduced law and order into his kingdom. He kept his money in coffers and taxed the people. He instituted a poll-tax, tolls for walking and driving, and a tax on shoes and stockings and dress trimmings. And whatever he wished for he got. For the sake of money, people brought him everything, and they offered to work for him, for everyone wanted money.

Iván the Fool, also, did not live badly. As soon as he had buried his father-in-law, he took off all his royal robes and gave them to his wife to put away in a chest. Once again he donned his hempen shirt, his breeches and peasant shoes, and started again to work.

"It's dull for me," he said. "I'm getting fat and have lost my appetite and my sleep." So he brought his father and mother and his deaf and dumb sister to live with him, and he worked as before.

People said, "But you are a king!"

"Yes," said he, "but even a king must eat."

One of his ministers came to him and said, "We have no money to pay salaries."

"All right," said Iván. "Then don't pay them."

"Then no one will serve."

"All right. Let them not serve. They will have more time to work; let them cart manure. There is plenty of scavenging to be done."

And people came to Iván to be tried. One said, "He stole my money." And Iván said, "All right, that shows that he wanted it."

And they all got to know that Iván was a fool. And his wife said to him, "People say that you are a fool."

"All right," said Iván.

His wife thought and thought about it, but she also was a fool.

"Shall I go against my husband? Where the needle goes the thread follows," she said.

So she took off her royal dress, put it away in a chest, and went to Iván's sister to learn to work. And she learned to work and began to help her husband.

And all the wise men left Iván's kingdom; only the fools remained.

Nobody had money. They lived and worked. They fed themselves and they fed others.

Part 10

The old Devil waited and waited for news from the imps of their having ruined the three brothers. But no news came. So he went himself to inquire about it. He searched and searched, but instead of finding the three imps he found only the three holes.

"Evidently they have failed," he thought. "I shall have to tackle it myself."

So he went to look for the brothers, but they were no longer in their old places. He found them in three different kingdoms. All three were living and reigning. This annoyed the old Devil very much.

"Well," he said, "I must try my own hand at the job."

First he went to King Simon. He did not go to him in his own shape, but disguised himself as a general, and drove to Simon's palace.

"I hear, King Simon," said the Devil, "that you are a great warrior, and as I know that business well, I desire to serve you."

King Simon questioned him, and seeing that he was a wise man, took him into his service.

The new commander began to teach King Simon how to form a strong army.

"First," he said, "we must levy more soldiers, for there are in your kingdom many people unemployed. We must recruit all the young men without exception. Then you will have five times as many soldiers as formerly. Secondly, we must get new rifles and cannons. I will introduce rifles that will fire a hundred balls at once which will fly out like peas. And I will get cannons that will consume with fire either man, or horse, or wall. They will burn up everything!"

Simon the King listened to the new commander, ordered all young men without exception to be enrolled as soldiers, and had new factories built in which he manufactured large quantities of improved rifles and cannons. Then he made haste to declare war against a neighboring king. As soon as he met the other army, King Simon ordered his soldiers to rain balls against it and shoot fire from the cannons, and at one blow he burned and crippled half the enemy's army. The neighboring king was so thoroughly frightened that he gave way and surrendered his kingdom. King Simon was delighted.

"Now," said Simon, "I will conquer the king of India."

But the Indian king had heard about King Simon, and had adopted all his inventions, and added more of his own. The Indian king enlisted not only all the young men, but all the single women also, and got together a greater army even than King Simon's. And he copied all King Simon's rifles and cannons, and invented a way of flying through the air to throw explosive bombs from above.

King Simon set out to fight the Indian king, expecting to beat him as he had beaten the other king, but the scythe that had cut so well had lost its edge. The king of India did not let Simon's army come within gunshot, but sent his women through the air to hurl down explosive bombs on to Simon's army. The women began to rain down bombs on the army like borax upon cockroaches. The army ran away and Simon the King was left alone. So the Indian king took Simon's kingdom, and Simon the Soldier fled as best he might.

Having finished with this brother, the old Devil went to King Tarás. Changing himself into a merchant, he settled in Tarás's kingdom, started a house of business, and began spending money. He paid high prices for everything, and everybody hurried to the new merchant's house to get money. And so much money spread among the people that they began to pay all their taxes promptly, and paid up all their debts, and King Tarás rejoiced.

"Thanks to the new merchant," thought Tarás, "I shall have more money than ever, and my life will be yet more comfortable."

And King Tarás began to form fresh plans and began to build a new palace. He gave notice that people should bring him wood and stone, and come to work, and he fixed high prices for everything. King Tarás thought people would come in crowds to work as before, but to his surprise, all the wood and stone was taken to the new merchant, and all the workmen went there, too. King Tarás increased his price, but the merchant bid yet more. King Tarás had much money, but the merchant had still more and outbid the king at every point.

And so the king's palace was at a standstill, and the building did not get on.

King Tarás planned a garden, and when autumn came he called for the people to come and plant the garden, but nobody came. All the people were engaged in digging a pond for the merchant. Winter came, and King Tarás wanted to buy sable furs for a new overcoat. He sent to buy them, but the messengers returned and said, "There are no sables left. The merchant has all the furs. He gave the best price and made carpets of the skins."

King Tarás wanted to buy some stallions. He sent to buy them, but the messengers returned saying, "The merchant has all the good stallions; they are carrying water to fill his pond."

All the king's affairs came to a standstill. Nobody would work for him, for everyone was busy working for the merchant, and they only brought King Tarás the merchant's money to pay their taxes.

King Tarás collected so much money that he had nowhere to store it, and his life became wretched. He ceased to form plans, and would have been glad enough simply to live, but he was hardly able even to do that. He ran short of everything. One after another his cooks, coachmen, and servants left him to go to the merchant. Soon he lacked even food. When he sent to the market to buy anything, there was nothing to be got, for the merchant had bought up everything, and people only brought the king money to pay their taxes.

Tarás the King got angry and banished the merchant from the country. But the merchant settled just across the frontier, and went on as before. For the sake of the merchant's money, people took everything to him instead of to the King.

Things went badly with King Tarás. For days together he had nothing to eat, and a rumor even got about that the merchant was boasting that he would buy up the king himself! King Tarás got frightened and did not know what to do.

At this time Simon the Soldier came to him, saying, "Help me, for the king of India has conquered me."

But King Tarás himself was completely overwhelmed with difficulties. "I myself," said he, "have had nothing to eat for two days."

Part II

Having done with the two brothers, the old Devil went to King Iván. He changed himself into a military general, and coming to Iván, he began to persuade him that he ought to have an army.

"It does not become a king," said the general, "to be without an army. Only give me the order, and I will collect soldiers from among your people and form one."

Iván listened to him. "All right," said Iván, "form an army, and teach them to sing songs well. I like to hear them do that."

So the old Devil went through Iván's kingdom to enlist men. He told them to go and be entered as soldiers, and that each should have a quart of spirits and a fine red cap.

The people laughed.

"We have plenty of spirits," they said. "We make it ourselves. And as for caps, the women make all kinds of them, even striped ones with tassels."

So nobody would enlist.

The old Devil came to Iván and said: "Your fools won't enlist of their own free will. We shall have to make them."

"All right," said Iván, "you can try."

So the old Devil gave notice that all the people were to enlist, and that Iván would put to death anyone who refused.

The people came to the general and said, "You say that if we do not go as soldiers, the king will put us to death, but you don't say what will happen if we do enlist. We have heard it said that soldiers get killed!"

"Yes, that happens sometimes."

When the people heard this they became obstinate.

"We won't go," they said. "Better meet death at home. Either way we must die."

"Fools! You are fools!" said the old Devil. "A soldier may be killed or he may not, but if you don't go, King Iván will have you killed for certain."

The people were puzzled and went to Iván the Fool to consult him.

"A general has come," said they, "who says we must all become soldiers. 'If you go as soldiers,' says he, 'you may be killed or you may not, but if you don't go, King Iván will certainly kill you.' Is this true?"

Iván laughed and said, "How can I, alone, put all you to death? If I were not a fool I would explain it to you, but as it is, I don't understand it myself."

"Then," said they, "we will not serve."

"All right," said Ivan. "Don't."

So the people went to the general and refused to enlist. And the old Devil saw that this game was up, and he went off and ingratiated himself with the king of Tarakán.

"Let us make war," he said, "and conquer King Iván's country. It is true there is no money, but there is plenty of corn and cattle and everything else."

So the king of Tarakán prepared to make war. He mustered a great army, provided rifles and cannons, marched to the frontier, and entered Iván's kingdom.

And people came to Iván and said, "The king of Tarakán is coming to make war on us."

"All right," said Iván, "let him come."

Having crossed the frontier, the king of Tarakán sent out his scouts to look for Iván's army. They looked and looked, but there was no army! They waited and waited for one to appear somewhere, but there were no signs of an army, and nobody to fight with. The king of Tarakán then sent them to seize the villages. The soldiers came to a village, and the people, both men and women, rushed out in astonishment to stare at the soldiers. The soldiers began to take their corn and cattle; the people let them have it, and did not resist. The soldiers went on to another village, and the same thing happened again. The soldiers went on for one day, then for two days, and everywhere the same thing happened. The people let them have everything, and no one resisted, but only invited the soldiers to live with them.

"Poor fellows," the people said, "if you have a hard life in your own land, why don't you come and stay with us altogether?"

The soldiers marched and marched, and still found no army. They only found people living and feeding themselves and others. Instead of resisting, they invited the soldiers to stay and live with them. The soldiers found it dull work, and so they came to the king of Tarakán and said, "We cannot fight here. Lead us elsewhere. War is all right, but what is this? It is like cutting pea soup! We will not make war here anymore."

The king of Tarakán grew angry and ordered his soldiers to over-run the whole kingdom, to destroy the villages, to burn the grain and the houses, and to slaughter the cattle. "And if you do not obey my orders," said he, "I will execute you all."

The soldiers were frightened, and began to act according to the King's orders. They began to burn houses and corn, and to kill cattle. But the fools still offered no resistance and only wept. The old men wept, the old women wept, and the young people wept.

"Why do you harm us?" they said. "Why do you waste good things? If you need them, why do you not take them for yourselves?"

At last the soldiers could stand it no longer. They refused to go any further, and the army disbanded and fled.

Part 12

The old Devil had to give it up. He could not get the better of Iván with soldiers. So he changed himself into a fine gentleman, and settled down in Iván's kingdom. He meant to overcome him by means of money, as he had overcome Tarás the Stout.

"I wish to do you a good turn, to teach you sense and reason. I will build a house among you and organize a trade."

"All right," said Iván, "come and live among us if you like."

The next morning the fine gentleman went out into the public square with a big sack of gold and a sheet of paper and said, "You all live like swine. I wish to teach you how to live properly. Build me a house according to this plan. You shall work as I instruct you, and I will pay you with gold coins." And he showed them the gold.

The fools were astonished. There was no money in use among them, as they bartered their goods and paid one another with labor. They looked at the gold coins with surprise.

"What nice little things they are!" they said.

And they began to exchange their goods and labor for the gentleman's gold pieces. And the old Devil began, as in Tarás's kingdom, to be free with his gold, and the people began to exchange everything for gold and to do all sorts of work for it.

The old Devil was delighted, and thought to himself, "Things are going right this time. Now I shall ruin the Fool as I did Tarás, and I shall buy him up body and soul."

But as soon as the fools had provided themselves with gold pieces, they gave them to the women for necklaces. The lasses plaited them into their tresses and at last the children in the street began to play with the little pieces. Everybody had plenty of them and they stopped taking them. But the fine gentleman's mansion was not yet half-built, and the grain and cattle for the year were not yet provided. So he gave notice that he wished people to come and work for him, and that he wanted cattle and grain. For each item and for each service he was ready to give many more pieces of gold.

But nobody came to work and nothing was brought. Only sometimes a boy or a little girl would run up to exchange an egg for a gold coin, but nobody else came, and he had nothing to eat. And being hungry, the fine gentleman went through the village to try and buy something for dinner. He tried at one house, offering a gold piece for a fowl, but the housewife wouldn't take it.

"I have a lot already," she said.

He tried at a widow's house to buy a herring, and offered a gold piece.

"I don't want it, my good sir," said she. "I have no children to play with it, and I myself already have three coins as curiosities."

He tried at a peasant's house to get bread, but neither would the peasant take money.

"I don't need it," said he, "but if you are begging 'for Christ's sake,' wait a bit and I'll tell the housewife to cut you a piece of bread."

At that the Devil spat and ran away. To hear Christ's name mentioned, let alone receiving anything for Christ's sake, hurt him more than sticking a knife into him.

And so he got no bread. Everyone had gold, and no matter where the old Devil went, nobody would give anything for money, but every one said, "Either bring something else, or come and work, or receive what you want in charity for Christ's sake."

But the old Devil had nothing but money, since he had no liking for work, and as for taking anything 'for Christ's sake,' he could not do that. And so the old Devil grew very angry.

"What more do you want when I give you money?" said he. "You can buy everything with gold and hire any kind of laborer." But the fools did not heed him.

"No, we do not want money," they said. "We have no payments to make and no taxes, so what should we do with it?"

The old Devil finally laid down to sleep without any supper.

The affair was told to Iván the Fool. People came and asked him, "What are we to do? A fine gentleman has turned up who likes to eat and drink and dress well, but he does not like to work, does not beg in Christ's name, but only offers gold pieces to everyone. At first people gave him all he wanted, until they had plenty of gold pieces, but now no one gives him anything. What's to be done with him? He will die of hunger before long."

Iván listened.

"All right," he said. "We must feed him. Let him live by turn at each house as a shepherd does to earn his room and board."

There was no help for it. The old Devil had to begin making the rounds.

In due course the turn came for him to go to Iván's house. The old Devil came in to dinner, and the deaf and dumb girl was getting it ready.

She had often been deceived by lazy folk who came early to dinner (that is, those who had not done their share of work and who ate up all the porridge), so it had occurred to her to find out the sluggards by their hands. Those who had rough hands, she put at the table, but the others with smooth hands got only the leftover scraps.

The old Devil sat down at the table, but the dumb girl seized him by the hands and looked at them. She saw that there were no hard or rough places there; the hands were clean and smooth, with long nails. The dumb girl gave a grunt and pulled the Devil away from the table. And Iván's wife said to him, "Don't be offended, fine gentleman. My sister-in-law does not allow anyone to come to table who does not have rough hands. But wait awhile, after the folk have eaten you shall have what is left."

The old Devil was offended that in the king's house they wished to feed him like a pig. He said to Iván, "It is a foolish law you have in your kingdom that everyone must work with his hands. It is your stupidity that invented it. Do people work only with their hands? What do you think wise men work with?"

And Iván said, "How are we fools to know? We do most of our work with our hands and our backs."

"That is because you are fools! But I will teach you how to work with the head. Then you will know that it is more profitable to work with the head than with the hands."

Iván was surprised.

"If that is so," he said, "then there is some sense in calling us fools!"

And the old Devil went on. "Only it is not easy to work with one's head. You give me nothing to eat, because I have no hard places on my hands, but you do not know that it is a hundred times more difficult to work with the head. Sometimes one's head quite splits."

Iván became thoughtful.

"Why, then, friend, do you torture yourself so? Is it pleasant when the head splits? Would it not be better to do easier work with your hands and your back?"

But the Devil said, "I do it all out of pity for you fools. If I didn't torture myself you would remain fools forever. But, having worked with my head, I can now teach you."

Iván was surprised.

"Do teach us!" said he, "so that when our hands get cramped we may use our heads for a change."

And the Devil promised to teach the people. So Iván gave notice throughout the kingdom that a fine gentleman had come who would teach everybody how to work with their heads, and that with the head more could be done than with the hands, and that the people ought all to come and learn.

Now there was in Iván's kingdom a high tower with many steps leading up to a lantern on the top. And Iván took the gentleman up there that everyone might see him.

So the gentleman took his place on the top of the tower and began to speak, and the people came together to see him. They thought the gentleman would really show them how to work with the head without using the hands. But the old Devil only taught them in many words how they might live without working. The people could make nothing of it. They looked and considered, and at last went off to attend to their affairs.

The old Devil stood on the tower a whole day, and did the same on a second day, talking all the time. But standing there so long he grew hungry, and the fools never thought of taking food to him up in the tower. They thought that if he could work with his head better than with his hands, he could at any rate easily provide himself with bread.

The old Devil stood on the top of the tower yet another day, talking away. People came near, looked on for a while, and then went away.

And Iván asked, "Well, has the gentleman begun to work with his head yet?"

"Not yet," said the people. "He's still spouting away."

The old Devil stood on the tower one day more, but he began to grow weak, and thus he staggered and hit his head against one of the pillars of the lantern. One of the people noticed it and told Iván's wife, and she ran to her husband who was in the field.

"Come and look," said she. "They say the gentleman is beginning to work with his head."

Iván was surprised.

"Really?" he said. Iván turned his horse around and went to the tower. And by the time he reached the tower the old Devil was quite exhausted with hunger, staggering and knocking his head against the pillars. And just as Iván arrived at the tower, the Devil stumbled, fell, and came bump,

bump, bump, straight down the stairs to the bottom, counting each step with a knock on his head!

"Well!" says Iván, "the fine gentleman told the truth when he said that 'sometimes one's head quite splits.' This is worse than blisters; after such work there will be swellings on the head."

The old Devil tumbled out at the foot of the stairs and struck his head against the ground. Iván was about to go up to him to see how much work he had done, when suddenly the earth opened and the old Devil fell through. Only a hole was left.

Iván scratched his head.

"What a nasty thing," he said. "It's one of those devils again! What a whopper! He must be the father of them all."

Iván is still living, and people crowd to his kingdom. His own brothers have come to live with him, and he feeds them, too. To everyone who comes and says, "Give me food!" Iván says, "All right. You can stay with us; we have plenty of everything."

Only there is one special custom in his kingdom. Whoever has rough hands comes to table, but whoever has not, must eat what the others leave.

Esarhaddon, King of Assyria

The Assyrian king, Esarhaddon, had conquered the kingdom of King Lailie, had destroyed and burnt the towns, taken all the inhabitants captive to his own country, slaughtered the warriors, beheaded some chieftains and impaled or flayed others, and had confined King Lailie himself in a cage.

As he lay on his bed one night, King Esarhaddon was thinking how he should execute Lailie, when suddenly he heard a rustling near his bed, and opening his eyes, he saw an old man with a long gray beard and mild eyes.

"You wish to execute Lailie?" asked the old man.

"Yes'" answered the king. "But I cannot make up my mind how to do it."

"But you are Lailie," said the old man.

"That's not true," replied the king. "Lailie is Lailie, and I am I."

"You and Lailie are one," said the old man. "You only imagine you are not Lailie, and that Lailie is not you."

"What do you mean by that?" said the king. "Here am I, lying on a soft bed, and around me are obedient men-slaves and women-slaves; tomorrow I shall feast with my friends as I did today. Lailie, however, is sitting like a bird in a cage, and tomorrow he will be impaled, his tongue will be hanging out as he struggles until he dies, and then his body will be torn in pieces by dogs."

"You cannot destroy his life," said the old man.

"And how about the fourteen thousand warriors I killed, with whose bodies I built a mound?" said the king. "I am alive, but they no longer exist. Does not that prove that I can destroy life?"

"How do you know they no longer exist?"

"Because I no longer see them. And, above all, they were tormented, but I was not. It was ill for them, but well for me."

"That, also, only seems so to you. You tortured yourself, but not them."

"I do not understand," said the king.

"Do you wish to understand?"

"Yes, I do."

"Then come here," said the old man, pointing to a large font full of water.

The king rose and approached the font.

"Strip, and enter the font."

Esarhaddon did as the old man bade him.

"As soon as I begin to pour this water over you," said the old man, filling a pitcher with the water, "dip down your head."

The old man tilted the pitcher over the king's head, and the king bent his head until it was under water.

And as soon as King Esarhaddon was under the water, he felt that he was no longer Esarhaddon, but someone else. And, feeling himself to be that other man, he saw himself lying on a rich bed beside a beautiful woman. He had never seen her before, but he knew she was his wife. The woman raised herself and said to him:

"Dear husband, Lailie! You were wearied by yesterday's work and have slept longer than usual, and I have guarded your rest and have not roused you. But now all of the princes await you in the Great Hall. Dress and go out to them."

And Esarhaddon, understanding from these words that he was Lailie, and not feeling at all surprised at this, but only wondering that he did not know it before, rose, dressed, and went into the Great Hall where the princes awaited him.

The princes greeted Lailie, their king, bowing to the ground, and then they rose, and at his word they sat down before him. Then the eldest of the princes began to speak, saying that it was impossible to endure any longer the insults of the wicked King Esarhaddon, and that they must make war on him. But Lailie disagreed, and gave orders that envoys shall be sent to remonstrate with King Esarhaddon, and thus he dismissed the princes from the audience. Afterwards he appointed men of note to act as ambassadors, and impressed on them what they were to say to King Esarhaddon.

Having finished this business, Esarhaddon, feeling himself to be Lailie, rode out to hunt wild asses. The hunt was successful. He killed two wild asses himself, and, having returned home, feasted with his friends, and witnessed a dance of slave girls. The next day he went to the court where he was awaited by petitioners, suitors, and prisoners brought for trial, and there as usual he decided the cases submitted to him. Having finished this business, he again rode out to his favorite amusement: the hunt. And again he was successful, this time killing with his own hand an old lioness and capturing her two cubs. After the hunt he again feasted with his friends, and was entertained with music and dances, and the night he spent with the wife whom he loved.

So, dividing his time between kingly duties and pleasures, he lived for days and weeks, awaiting the return of the ambassadors he had sent to that King Esarhaddon who used to be himself. Not until a month had passed did the ambassadors return, and they returned with their noses and ears cut off.

King Esarhaddon had ordered the ambassadors to tell Lailie that what had been done to them would be done to King Lailie himself also, unless he sent immediately a tribute of silver, gold, and cypress-wood, and came himself to pay homage to King Esarhaddon.

Lailie, formerly Esarhaddon, again assembled the princes and took counsel with them as to what he should do. They all with one accord said that war must be made against Esarhaddon, without waiting for him to attack them. King Lailie agreed. Taking his place at the head of the army, he started on the campaign. The campaign lasted seven days. Each day the king rode around the army to rouse the courage of his warriors. On the eighth day his army met that of Esarhaddon in a broad valley through which a river flowed. Lailie's army fought bravely, but Lailie, formerly Esarhaddon, saw the enemy swarming down from the mountains like ants, overrunning the valley and overwhelming his army; and, in his chariot, he flung himself into the midst of the battle, hewing and felling the enemy. But the warriors of Lailie were but as hundreds, while those of Esarhaddon were as thousands; and Lailie felt himself wounded and taken prisoner. Nine days he journeyed with other captives, bound, and guarded by the warriors of Esarhaddon.

On the tenth day he reached Nineveh and was placed in a cage. Lailie suffered not so much from hunger and from his wound as from shame and impotent rage. He felt how powerless he was to avenge himself on his enemy for all he was suffering. All he could do was to deprive his enemies of the pleasure of seeing his sufferings, and so he firmly resolved to endure courageously, without a murmur, all they could do to him. For twenty days he sat in his cage, awaiting execution. He saw his relatives and friends led out to death. He heard the groans of those who were executed; some had their hands and feet cut off, others were flayed alive, but he showed neither disquietude, nor pity, nor fear. He saw the wife he loved, bound, and led by two black eunuchs. He knew she was being taken as a slave to Esarhaddon. That, too, he bore without a murmur. But one of the guards placed to watch him said, "I pity you, Lailie. You were a king, but what are you now?" And hearing these words, Lailie remembered all he had lost. He clutched the bars of his cage, and, wishing to kill himself, beat his head against them. But he had not the strength to do so, and, groaning in despair, he fell upon the floor of his cage.

At last two executioners opened his cage door, and having strapped his arms tight behind him, they led him to the place of execution which was soaked with blood. Lailie saw a sharp stake dripping with blood, from which the corpse of one of his friends had just been torn, and he understood that this had been done that the stake might serve for his own execution. They stripped Lailie of his clothes. He was startled at the leanness of his once strong, handsome body. The two executioners seized that body by its lean thighs; they lifted him up and were about to let him fall upon the stake.

"This is death and destruction!" thought Lailie, and, forgetful of his resolve to remain bravely calm to the end, he sobbed and prayed for mercy. But no one listened to him.

"But this cannot be," thought he. "Surely I am asleep. It is a dream." And he made an effort to rouse himself, and did indeed awake, only to find himself neither Esarhaddon nor Lailie, but some kind of an animal. He was astonished that he was an animal, and astonished, also, at not having known this before.

He was grazing in a valley, tearing the tender grass with his teeth, and brushing away flies with his long tail. Around him was frolicking a long-legged, dark-gray ass-colt, striped down its back. Kicking up its hind legs, the colt galloped full speed to Esarhaddon, and poking him under the stomach with its smooth little muzzle, searched for the teat, and, finding it, quieted down, swallowing regularly. Esarhaddon understood that he was a she-ass, the colt's mother, and this neither surprised nor grieved him, but rather gave him pleasure. He experienced a glad feeling of simultaneous life in himself and in his offspring.

But suddenly something flew near with a whistling sound and hit him in the side, and with its sharp point entered his skin and flesh. Feeling a burning pain, Esarhaddon (who was at the same time the ass) tore the udder from the colt's teeth, and laying back his ears galloped to the herd from which he had strayed. The colt kept up with him, galloping by his side. They had already nearly reached the herd, which had started off, when another arrow in full flight struck the colt's neck. It pierced the skin and quivered in its flesh. The colt sobbed piteously and fell upon its knees. Esarhaddon could not abandon it, and remained standing over it. The colt rose, tottered on its long, thin legs, and again fell. A fearful two-legged being, a man, ran up and cut its throat.

"This cannot be; it is still a dream!" thought Esarhaddon, as he made a last effort to awake. "Surely I am not Lailie, nor the ass, but Esarhaddon!"

He cried out, and at the same instant lifted his head out of the font. The old man was standing beside him, pouring over his head the last drops from the pitcher.

"Oh, how terribly I have suffered! And for how long!" said Esarhaddon.

"Long?" replied the old man. "You have only dipped your head under water and lifted it again. See, the water is not yet all out of the pitcher. Do you now understand?"

Esarhaddon did not reply, but only looked at the old man with terror.

"Do you now understand," continued the old man, "that Lailie is you, and the warriors you put to death were you also? And not the warriors only, but the animals which you slew when hunting and ate at your feasts were also you. You thought life dwelt in you alone, but I have drawn aside the veil of delusion and have let you see that by doing evil to others you have done it to yourself also. Life is unified in them all, and your life is but a portion of this same common life. And only in that one part of life that is yours can you make life better or worse, increasing or decreasing it. You can only improve life in yourself by destroying the barriers that divide your life from that of others, and by considering others as yourself, and by loving them. By so doing you increase your share of life. You injure your life when you think of it as the only life, trying to add to its welfare at the expense of other lives. By so doing you only lessen it. To destroy the life that dwells in others is beyond your power. The life of those you have slain has vanished from your eyes, but it is not destroyed. You thought to lengthen your own life and to shorten theirs, but you cannot do this. Life knows neither time nor space. The life of a moment and the life of a thousand years: your life, and the life of all the visible and invisible beings in the world, are equal. To destroy life, or to alter it, is impossible, for life is the one thing that exists. Everything else only seems to be."

Having said this the old man vanished.

The next morning King Esarhaddon gave orders that Lailie and all the prisoners should be set at liberty and that the executions should cease.

On the third day he called his son Assurbanipal, and gave the kingdom over into his hands. Lailie himself went into the desert to think over all he had learnt. Afterwards he went about as a wanderer through the towns and villages, preaching to the people that all life is one, and that when men wish to harm others, they really do evil to themselves.

A Grain as Big as a Hen's Egg

One day some children found, in a ravine, a thing shaped like a grain of corn, with a groove down the middle, but as large as a hen's egg. A traveler passing by saw the thing, bought it from the children for a penny, and taking it to town sold it to the king as a curiosity.

The king called together his wise men and told them to find out what the thing was. The wise men pondered and pondered and could not make head or tail of it, until one day, when the thing was lying on a window-sill, a hen flew in and pecked at it till she made a hole in it, and then everyone saw that it was a grain of corn. The wise men went to the king, and said:

"It is a grain of corn."

At this the king was much surprised, and he ordered the learned men to find out when and where such corn had grown. The learned men pondered again, and searched in their books, but could find nothing about it. So they returned to the king and said:

"We can give you no answer. There is nothing about it in our books. You will have to ask the peasants. Perhaps some of them may have heard from their fathers when and where grain grew to such a size."

So the king gave orders that some very old peasant should be brought before him, and so his servants found such a man and brought him to the king. Old and bent, ashy pale and toothless, he just managed with the help of two crutches to totter into the king's presence.

The king showed him the grain, but the old man could hardly see it. He took it, however, and felt it with his hands. The king questioned him, saying:

"Can you tell us, old man, where such grain as this grew? Have you ever bought such corn or sown such in your fields?"

The old man was so deaf that he could hardly hear what the king said and only understood with great difficulty.

"No!" he answered at last. "I never sowed nor reaped any like it in my fields, nor did I ever buy any grain such as this. When we bought corn, the grains were always as small as they are now. But you might ask my father. He may have heard where such grain grew."

So the king sent for the old man's father, and he was found and brought before the king. He came walking with one crutch. The king showed him the grain, and the old peasant, who was still able to see, took a good look at it. And the king asked him:

"Can you not tell us, old man, where corn like this used to grow? Have you ever bought any like it, or sown any in your fields?"

Though the old man was rather hard of hearing, he still heard better than his son had done.

"No," he said. "I never sowed nor reaped any grain like this in my field. As to buying, I never bought any, for in my time money was not yet in use. Everyone grew his own corn, and when there was any need we shared with one another. I do not know where corn like this grew. Ours was larger and yielded more flour than present-day grain, but I never saw any like this. I have, however, heard my father say that in his time the grain grew larger and yielded more flour than ours. You had better ask him."

So the king sent for this old man's father, and they found him, too, and brought him before the king. He entered walking easily and without crutches. His eye was clear, his hearing good, and he spoke distinctly. The king showed him the grain and the old grandfather looked at it, turning it about in his hand.

"It is long since I saw such a fine grain," said he, and he bit a piece off and tasted it.

"It's the very same kind," he added.

"Tell me, grandfather," said the king, "when and where was such corn grown? Have you ever bought any like it or sown any in your fields?"

And the old man replied: "Corn like this used to grow everywhere in my time. I lived on corn like this in my young days and fed others on it. It was grain like this that we used to sow and reap and thresh."

And the king asked, "Tell me, grandfather, did you buy it anywhere, or did you grow it all yourself?"

The old man smiled.

"In my time," he answered, "no one ever thought of such a sin as buying or selling bread. And we knew nothing of money. Each man had corn enough of his own."

"Then tell me, grandfather," asked the king, "where was your field; where did you grow corn like this?"

And the grandfather answered: "My field was God's earth. Wherever I plowed, there was my field. Land was free. It was a thing no man called his own. Labor was the only thing men called their own."

"Answer me two more questions," said the king. "The first is, 'Why did the earth bear such grain then, and has ceased to do so now?' And the second is, 'Why does your grandson walk with two crutches, your son with one, and you yourself with none? Your eyes are bright, your teeth sound, and your speech clear and pleasant to the ear. How have these things come about?'"

And the old man answered: "These things are so because men have ceased to live by their own labor and have taken to depending on the labor of others. In the old time, men lived according to God's law. They had what was their own and coveted not what others had produced."

Three Questions

It once occurred to a certain king that if he always knew the right time to begin everything, if he knew who were the right people to listen to, and whom to avoid, and, above all, if he always knew what was the most important thing to do, he would never fail in anything he might undertake.

And this thought having occurred to him, he had it proclaimed throughout his kingdom that he would give a great reward to anyone who would teach him what was the right time for every action, and who were the most necessary people, and how he might know what was the most important thing to do.

And learned men came to the king, but they all answered his questions differently.

In reply to the first question, some said that to know the right time for every action, one must draw up in advance a table of days, months and years, and must live strictly according to it. Only thus, said they, could everything be done at its proper time. Others declared that it was impossible to decide beforehand the right time for every action, but that, not letting oneself be absorbed in idle pastimes, one should always attend to all that was going on, and then do what was most needful. Others, again, said that however attentive the king might be to what was going on, it was impossible for one man to decide correctly the right time for every action, but that he should have a council of wise men who would help him to fix the proper time for everything.

But then again others said there were some things which could not wait to be laid before a council, but about which one had at once to decide whether to undertake them or not. But in order to decide that, one must know beforehand what was going to happen. It is only magicians who know that, and therefore, in order to know the right time for every action, one must consult magicians.

Equally various were the answers to the second question. Some said the people that the king most needed were his councilors; others said, the priests; others, the doctors; and finally, some said the warriors were the most necessary.

To the third question, as to what was the most important occupation, some replied that the most important thing in the world was science. Others said it was skill in warfare, and some said it was religious worship.

All the answers being different, the king agreed with none of them and gave the reward to none. But still wishing to find the right answers to his questions, he decided to consult a hermit, widely renowned for his wisdom.

The hermit lived in a wood which he never left, and he received none but common folk. So the king put on simple clothes, and before reaching the hermit's cell dismounted from his horse, and, leaving his bodyguard behind, went on alone.

When the king approached, the hermit was digging the ground in front of his hut. Seeing the king, he greeted him and went on digging. The hermit was frail and weak, and each time he stuck his spade into the ground and turned a little earth, he breathed heavily.

The king went up to him and said, "I have come to you, wise hermit, to ask you to answer three questions: How can I learn to do the right thing at the right time? Who are the people I most need, and to whom should I, therefore, pay more attention than to the rest? And, thirdly, what affairs are the most important and need my first attention?"

The hermit listened to the king, but answered nothing. He just spat on his hand and continued digging.

"You are tired," said the king. "Let me take the spade and work awhile for you."

"Thanks!" said the hermit, and, giving the spade to the king, he sat down on the ground.

When he had dug two beds, the king stopped and repeated his questions. The hermit again gave no answer, but rose, stretched out his hand for the spade, and said:

"Now rest awhile and let me work a bit."

But the king did not give him the spade, and continued to dig. One hour passed, and another. The sun began to sink behind the trees, and the king at last stuck the spade into the ground, and said:

"I came to you, wise man, for an answer to my questions. If you can give me none, tell me so, and I will return home."

"Here comes someone running," said the hermit. "Let us see who it is." The king turned round and saw a bearded man come running out of the wood. The man held his hands pressed against his stomach, and blood was flowing from under them. When he reached the king, he fell fainting on the ground moaning feebly. The king and the hermit unfastened the man's clothing. There was a large wound in his stomach. The king washed it as best he could, and bandaged it with his handkerchief and with a towel the hermit had. But the blood would not stop flowing, and so the king again and again removed the bandage soaked with warm blood, and washed and rebandaged the wound.

When at last the blood ceased flowing, the man revived and asked for something to drink. The king brought fresh water and gave it to him. Meanwhile the sun had set and it had become cool. So the king, with the hermit's help, carried the wounded man into the hut and laid him on the bed. Lying on the bed the man closed his eyes and was quiet. The king was so tired with his walk and with the work he had done, that he crouched down on the threshold and fell asleep. He slept so soundly all through the short summer night, that when he awoke in the morning, it was long before he could remember where he was, or who was the strange bearded man lying on the bed and gazing intently at him with shining eyes.

"Forgive me!" said the bearded man in a weak voice, when he saw that the king was awake and was looking at him.

"I do not know you and have nothing to forgive you for," said the king.

"You do not know me, but I know you. I am that enemy of yours who swore to revenge himself on you, because you executed his brother and seized his property. I knew you had gone alone to see the hermit, and I resolved to kill you on your way back. But the day passed and you did not return. So I came out from my ambush to find you, and I came upon your bodyguards, and they recognized me, and wounded me. I escaped from them, but should have bled to death had you not dressed my wound. I wished to kill you and you have saved my life. Now, if I live, and if you wish it, I will serve you as your most faithful slave and will bid my sons do the same. Forgive me!"

The king was very glad to have made peace with his enemy so easily and to have gained him for a friend, and he not only forgave him, but said he would send his servants and his own physician to attend him, and he promised to restore his property.

Having taken leave of the wounded man, the king went out into the porch and looked around for the hermit. Before going away he wished once more to beg an answer to the questions he had put. The hermit was outside, on his knees, sowing seeds in the beds that had been dug the day before.

The king approached him, and said:

"For the last time, I pray you to answer my questions, wise man."

"You have already been answered!" said the hermit still crouching on his thin legs, and looking up at the king who stood before him.

"How answered? What do you mean?" asked the king.

"Do you not see," replied the hermit. "If you had not pitied my weakness yesterday and had not dug those beds for me, but had gone your way, that man would have attacked you, and you would have repented of not having stayed with me. So the most important time was when you were digging the beds, and I was the most important man, and to do me good was your most important business. Afterwards when that man ran to us, the most important time was when you were attending to him, for if you had not bound up his wounds he would have died without having made peace with you. So he was the most important man, and what you did for him was your most important business. Remember then: there is only one time that is important—Now! It is the most important time because it is the only time when we have any real power. The most necessary man is he with whom you are, for no man knows whether he will ever have dealings with anyone else. And the most important affair is to do him good, because for that purpose alone was man sent into this life!"

Introducing *Holy Fool Arts*

Holy Fool Arts is a faith-based theatrical production company founded by Tevyn East and Jay Beck. Holy Fool Arts fuses earth-centered spirituality with the biblical prophetic tradition, and draws on the ancient power of art and ceremony to facilitate the healing work of communal grief, struggle, and defiant joy. Our main program offerings include the following:

- **Caravan**—touring works of theopoetic theater and earth-centered worship;

- **Beast**—a blues-infused music project that unearths the significance of wild nature within the Judeo-Christian tradition;

- **Leaps & Bounds**—a one-woman show that exposes the environmental and social costs of our growth-oriented economy;

- **Carnival de Resistance**—a traveling arts carnival, education initiative, and eco-village demonstration project.

For several years now, Holy Fool Arts has brought the Carnival de Resistance (as well as other artistic productions) to communities across the country. Incorporating music, drama, dance, and creative retellings of biblical stories for our time, Holy Fool Arts invites audiences to engage with the struggle for justice through embodied worship, creative play, alternative energy demonstrations, and political activism. We subvert narratives of capitalism, US imperialism and white supremacy while simultaneously embodying and nurturing alternative life-giving visions. We educate about the intersectionality of social and ecological justice issues, model transformative practices, and amplify local campaigns and community-rooted initiatives.

The work of Holy Fool Arts draws deeply from the Holy Fool tradition and honors the many ways that holy foolery continues today: through street protests, direct actions, theatrical experiments, and through churches intent on decolonizing their liturgy and re-indigenizing their faith tradition. The important work of pushing through illusions may be rooted in ancient traditions, but it continues to find new and radical expressions today.

At Holy Fool Arts, we celebrate the long history of this tradition by producing new creative offerings with ancient themes. We incorporate the feral theatricality of the Hebrew prophets into our performances; the Hebrew scripture is infused throughout with humor, and the prophets adopted clown-like behavior in their lifestyles as well as their messages. They ate bugs (Mark 1.6) and hid under bushes (Jonah 4.6–8); Isaiah walked around naked for three years (Isa. 20.2–3); Jeremiah smashed pots (Jer. 19.1–13) and wore a yoke on his neck (Jer. 28.10–16); Hosea married a prostitute; Ezekiel cooked his food by burning his own excrement (Ezek. 4.12) and ate a copy of ancient scripture (Ezek. 3.1–3). We are inspired by these prophetic acts of public pedagogy, and we believe Jesus himself embodied this tradition and taught this way.

We are especially drawn to the Holy Fool tradition as we see it exemplified in the radical life of Jesus. The topsy turvy narrative begins as Jesus is planted in his mother's womb. The "Magnificat" of the newly pregnant Mary, forever memorialized through feasts and carnivals, captures a vision populated by prophetic inversions:

> God is bringing the mighty down from their thrones,
>   exalting the lowly;
> filling the hungry with good things,
>   and sending the rich away empty" (Luke 1:52–53).

Even in orthodox traditions, the reversal symbolized by the "Jesus event" is apparent: the creator of the universe visits us as a refugee baby, born under the boot of empire to an unwed mother, and placed in an animal feeding trough with the lowly beasts around him.

Throughout his life as teacher-prophet, Jesus continues to flip the prevailing scripts of religious and cultural institutions, prefacing new teachings with, "You have heard it said, but *I* tell you. . ." He breaks taboos: Jesus disobeys his parents, assumes a child can teach his elders, gleans when he's not supposed to, and builds friendships with taxpayers, prostitutes, and zealots. All of his teachings are social monkey-wrenches and subversions: to save your life you have to lose it; the last will be first, the first will be last;

to enter the kingdom of heaven, you have to give everything to the poor. The teachings of Jesus recognize that the world is already upside down, and that the kingdom of God reverses, restores, and rights it.

Jesus was deeply embedded in the daily struggle of poor, ill, vulnerable, and outcast people. As Wes Nisker reminds us, "Identification with the poor almost inevitably forces the holy fool into the role of rebel, leading populist movements that shake up the existing political and spiritual orders. State and church tend to scratch each other's backs, and when you challenge one you threaten the other. The greatest of holy fools have been out of favor with the priesthood and often in trouble with the law."[1] This is why Jesus' crucifixion is not simply a symbol of Roman imperial torture and the squashing of insurrection; we must remember that he was also condemned and killed for blasphemy by the ruling scribes. The twist of the story unfolds, revealing that God is killed for sharing God's radical orientation. But don't be fooled; God's body rises, and even the grave is illuminated as the threshold to new life.

According to Olive Fleming Drane, a self-identified clown minister, the early church was a place where theatricality and holy foolery abounded. To understand the tradition of the Holy Fool, she reminds us that "the Church came to birth straddling two cultures, the Jewish and the Roman."[2] Both cultures had traditions of performative mockery, including prophets and mimes. And both, as Drane observes, "offered exaggerated images of reality as a way of getting to the real issues, often by exposing the hypocrisies and inconsistencies of public life."[3] Accounts of feasts and baptisms, redistribution of resources, and miraculous escapes in the book of Acts give us insight into the topsy turvy ways of the beloved community. And while Paul is remembered as a traveling apostle and tentmaker, there may be a hidden layer of theatricality within his skill set. Drane shares that 'tentmaker' (*skēnopoios*) "in other ancient texts. . .invariably refers not to tents but to the construction of theatrical scenery and costumes. When [Paul] recommended foolishness over wisdom, he may well have been doing so from personal experience – and his readers would almost certainly have

---

1. Wes Nisker, *The Essential Crazy Wisdom* (Toronto: Ten Speed Press, 2001), 57.

2. Olive Fleming Drane. "The holy fool: Clowning in Christian Ministry" Transmissions. Spring 2011, (https://www.biblesociety.org.uk/uploads/content/bible_in_transmission/files/2011_spring/BiT_Spring_2011_Drane.pdf), 17.

3. Ibid., 17.

seen it as an allusion to the public clowns who turned everything upside down in their passion for the truth (1 Cor. 1.18–25; 4.10)."[4]

Along with the Hebrew prophets, Jesus, and the leaders of the early church, Holy Fool Arts believes that the world is already upside down. To create the world we long for, we might just have to flip it over! This holy work goes beyond the faith-led efforts of progressive scholarship and justice-oriented conferences, and demands that we become embodied, imaginative, creative and disruptive.

Tevyn East and Jay Beck
April 2018
Philadelphia

For more information about Holy Fool Arts go to:

Holyfoolarts.org
Carnivalderesistance.com
facebook.com/HolyFoolArts/
info@holyfoolarts.org

4. Ibid., 17.